## DATE DUE

Remembering Barbara Niblett, who made
Burford Playgroup a happy place — J.W.

First American edition published in 2001 by Carolrhoda Books, Inc.

Text copyright © 2001 by Jeanne Willis. Illustrations copyright © 2001 by Mark Birchall.

Originally published in 2001 by Andersen Press, Ltd., London, England.

Carolrhoda Books, Inc., a division of Lerner Publishing Group
241 First Avenue North, Minneapolis, MN 55401 U.S.A.

Website address: www.lernerbooks.com

Library of Congress Cataloging-in-Publication Data

Willis, Jeanne.
    Be Gentle, Python! / by Jeanne Willis ; illustrated by Mark Birchall.—American ed.
      p. cm.
    Summary: On Python's first day of school, she can't stop squeezing her classmates, until Elephant
    accidently shows her how it feels.
    ISBN 1-57505-508-2 (lib. bdg. : alk. paper)
[1. Pythons—Fiction. 2. Snakes—Fiction. 3. Animals—Fiction. 4. First day of school—Fiction.
5. Schools—Fiction. 6. Behavior—Fiction.] I. Birchall, Mark, 1955– ill. II. Title.
PZ7.W68313 Bc 2001
[E]—dc21                        00-012345

Printed and bound in Singapore
1 2 3 4 5 6 - OS - 06 05 04 03 02 01

# Be Gentle, Python!

## By Jeanne Willis
## Pictures by Mark Birchall

Carolrhoda Books, Inc./Minneapolis

It was Python's first day at school.
"Be good," said her mother. And off she went.
"What shall I do now?" wondered Python.

"Find somebody to play with,"
said the teacher.
So Python went into the playhouse.

# Squeak! Squeak! Squeak! Squeak!

"Teacher! Tea . . . cher! Python is squeezing Rat!" shouted Weasel.

The teacher spoke very firmly to Python.
"You are not to squeeze," she said.
"Rat doesn't like it."
"What do I do now?" wondered Python.

"Story time," said the teacher. Everbody sat on the floor and listened quietly. Then, just as the story was getting to the exciting part...

# Squeal! Squeal! Squeal! Squeal!

"Teacher! Tea . . . cher! She's doing it again!" shouted Weasel.

The teacher stopped reading. She spoke very strictly to Python.

"You must not squeeze," she said. "It is unpleasant. Rabbit does **not** like it."

"What now?" wondered Python.

"Clay," said the teacher. "We're going to make colorful clay snakes."
Python went over to the clay table.
For a moment, all was quiet. Then there was the most terrible bellowing and harrumphing and hissing that you have ever heard!
"Teacher! Tea . . . cher!" shouted Weasel.
"What is it now? Is Python squeezing somebody?" asked the teacher.

"No, Teacher. Somebody is squeezing Python!"
It was Elephant.

"Python was lying on the table and I thought she was a piece of clay," Elephant explained.

After that, Python behaved beautifully.

Her mother arrived to take her home.
"How did she get along with the others?"
she asked the teacher.
"Oh ... very squeezily,"
the teacher said.